Crush

Jenna

The evening has gone better than I dared hope.

Everyone's fed, everyone's laughing, and the table is littered with empty wine bottles and scattered napkins. Grace looks radiant, Aaron is beaming, and the bridesmaids are tipsy enough to giggle at anything. Relief floods through me.

Maybe I can do this. Maybe I really am cut out for wedding planning.

This is the first event I've handled completely on my own since joining the company, and I've been terrified of slipping up. But tonight feels smooth, joyful, exactly what a rehearsal dinner should be. If tomorrow goes half as well, my boss will have nothing to complain about.

I should be basking in that small victory. But I'm not.

Because every time I glance across the room, Jack Westmore is already watching me.

And every time I catch him, it's like my body betrays me all over again.

My pulse kicks up, my breath shortens, and warmth coils low in my belly. He doesn't even try to hide the way his eyes track me, heavy and hungry, like I'm the only thing in the room worth looking at. Like he could devour me whole.

It makes my knees weak.

It also makes my breasts ache.

I swallow hard and force myself to stand up straighter, folding my arms across my chest. I shouldn't be thinking about that. Not when my body is already heavy and full, the swell of my breasts pressing uncomfortably against the bodice of my dress.

The truth is shameful enough: I'm twenty-two and overflowing with milk.

It started eighteen months ago, when my brother and his husband adopted a baby and worried that formula wouldn't be enough. I offered to help, and took herbs and used a pump multiple times a day to induce lactation. I didn't tell anyone how much I secretly loved it. How soothing and natural it felt to be able to provide something so vital. How feminine it made me feel. And I definitely didn't tell anyone that now I can't seem to stop, even though little baby Anna doesn't need my milk anymore. That I don't want to stop.

But that's exactly why a man like Jack Westmore could never actually want me if he knew the truth. He's older, powerful, perfect in every devastating way. From what Grace has told me, he runs his own very successful business in finance, and he's paid for everything for her big day.

And I'm just... me. Too young. Too inexperienced. And far, far too full of milk.

I drag my eyes away from him, cheeks hot, and force myself to focus on my job.

Which is exactly when Ryan, the best man, steps into my path.

Overflowing for the Father of the Bride

Willow Watkins

Copyright Page

Contents

Chapter One

Jack

The restaurant is too warm, too loud, and far too crowded with people I have little interest in making small talk with. But my daughter's happiness means I tolerate it.

"Dad, you're going to love her," Grace gushes beside me as we walk towards the private dining room. Her fiancé, Aaron, is on her other side, hand tucked at her back like he never wants to let her go. It makes me strangely proud to see how much he adores her, even if the kid still looks like he's barely out of college.

"She's incredible," Grace continues, her eyes glowing. "She's worked so hard for me this past year. Honestly, this whole wedding? It's all her. Jenna's the reason everything is exactly what I've dreamed of ever since I was a little girl. She even arranged everything for the rehearsal dinner tonight. I don't know what I would have done without her."

I nod and hum politely, but I don't care much about flowers and place settings. But if this wedding planner has made my only daughter happy, then I'm grateful to her. Grace is all I've had ever since her mom left me six years ago for a co-worker, so my daughter's happiness means the world to me.

The doors open and we step into the private room. A long table is dressed in white linen, crystal glasses catching the low golden light, bottles of wine already breathing. The bridal party is there, laughing too loud, full of nerves and champagne.

I let my attention drift, scanning faces, cataloguing exits, already thinking about when I can slip away for a bourbon at the bar.

And then she walks in.

My lungs seize. My blood turns molten.

She's... Christ. She's everything.

I've never seen her before, so I have to assume it's the wedding planner Grace hasn't been able to stop talking about. Her blonde hair is in a soft twist, and she's wearing a dress the color of cream that clings so damn sweetly to her curves. My heart hammers so hard in my chest I'm surprised Grace doesn't hear it.

I've never believed in instant anything. Not fate, not destiny, and definitely not love at first sight. But the moment that blonde beauty steps into the room, I know with a bone-deep certainty: *she's mine.*

Not mine someday. Not mine if circumstances align.

Mine now.

My daughter is still talking to Aaron beside me, completely oblivious to the chaos running through my mind and body right now. I barely hear her as Jenna moves across the room, greeting all the bridesmaids with soft hugs, and shakes hands with the groomsmen. She's polite and efficient; all professionalism until her eyes meet mine.

The world stutters.

Her smile falters, lips parting with surprise. A flush blooms high on her cheeks. And in that heartbeat of recognition, it's obvious she knows me the way I know her.

"Jenna!" Grace calls, tugging her over. My daughter's voice breaks the spell, but I can't unclench my jaw. My hands flex at my sides like they already ache to hold her, to pin her, to keep her where she belongs - beneath me, against me, with me always.

"Dad, this is Jenna Lane. Jenna, this is my father, Jack Westmore."

Her hand is small, delicate, when I take it. Soft as silk. I have to force myself not to crush it, not to yank her towards me like a starving man finally handed his first meal in years.

"It's a pleasure, sir," she says, her voice gentle, musical. She looks up at me through her lashes, and it's like she's pouring gasoline on my already burning chest.

"The pleasure's all mine," I rasp, and it's the truth. My voice comes out too low, too rough. Like I've already been inside her. Like I'm already ruined.

There's small talk. I couldn't repeat a word of it if you paid me. She's explaining something to Grace about table placements, meal choices, decor. All I can think about is the way her soft pink lips shape each word, how her throat moves when she swallows, the voluptuous swell of her breasts beneath that pretty dress. My body reacts with brutal speed, blood surging south until I'm hard as stone.

I can already taste her. Can already imagine how she'll sound when she cries my name, the way her breath will catch when I sink into her for the first time.

My daughter slips her hand into mine, tugging. "Dad, come on, it's time to sit down."

I let her lead me towards the table, but my eyes never leave Jenna. Not once. I glance back over my shoulder, and she's staring after me, her lips parted and her cheeks flushed, that luscious chest rising and falling too fast.

She feels it. I know she does.

Good.

Because there isn't a damn thing in this world that's going to stop me from making her mine.

We all take out seats at the long table. Crystal glasses clink, silverware shines, and the servers glide in and out with plates of food. Voices rise around me, full of laughter and nerves.

Grace leans towards Aaron, her eyes shining. "Can you believe the wedding is finally almost here?"

He picks up her hand from where it rests on the table and kisses the back of it. "I've been waiting for this day since the first time I saw you back in high school. I can't wait to put my ring on your finger at last."

One of the bridesmaids sighs, propping her chin on her hand. "You two are so disgustingly sweet. It's like watching a romance movie in real life."

Aaron's best man and best friend, Ryan, grins and raises his glass. "You should have seen them back when they first met. He used to write terrible poetry for her."

Grace laughs, cheeks turning pink.

"Don't tell people about that!" Aaron groans, but the table erupts in good-natured teasing.

I smile faintly, nod when appropriate, but my mind isn't on their chatter. My eyes are locked on Jenna.

She floats around the room like she's the one holding it all together. Soft words here, a reassuring touch there, always smiling, always attentive. She doesn't sit. She doesn't stop. She's making sure every detail is perfect, and I can't take my eyes off her.

Every step she takes, every tilt of her head, every time her lips curve into that sweet smile, my chest tightens. It's madness. I've known her for less than an hour, and I already know I'll never want another woman again.

She approaches our end of the table, leaning down to murmur something to Grace. Her scent, subtle and intoxicating, drifts over, and I grip the stem of my wineglass so I don't reach for her.

Ryan's gaze drops straight to her chest, and something hot and ugly spikes in me. He grins as if he's got a right to look at her that way. "Hi, gorgeous. Maybe you'll let me buy you a drink later?"

Jenna stiffens, though she covers it up with a polite smile. "That's kind, but I'm working tonight. I'll have to pass."

Anyone with half a brain can hear the edge in her voice, see the discomfort in her eyes. But Ryan just chuckles, leaning back with smug ease. "Playing hard to get, huh?"

She steps away before he can push further, retreating across the room.

Grace turns sharply to Ryan, frowning. "Knock it off. She's here for work, not to get hit on."

He shrugs, unbothered. "Relax. She liked it. Didn't you see how she blushed? Women just play coy because they like to be chased."

My jaw tightens until my teeth ache. I lean forward, my voice dropping into the kind of tone that men recognize, the kind that promises consequences. "She said no. Once. That's all it takes. Now leave her the fuck alone."

Ryan raises his brows, smirking like it's all a joke. "Fine. I'll back off. For now."

I hold his gaze until he looks away, his smirk faltering enough to tell me he heard the threat beneath my words.

Across the room, Jenna glances back. Her eyes find mine. She looks flustered, pink-cheeked, but there's something else there too. Heat. Longing. The same desperate pull that's ripping me apart.

I don't look away.

Because there's no chance in hell I'll let anyone else touch her. Not when I've finally found the woman meant to be mine. And not when she so clearly feels it too.

He plants a hand on the wall beside me, leaning in close enough that I can smell the stench of wine that clings to his breath. "Hey, gorgeous. You've been working so hard tonight. Why don't you let me buy you that drink now? You deserve some fun."

I take a step back, trying to keep my smile polite. "Thank you, but I really can't. I'm still working."

His grin widens, shark-like. "Come on. Just one drink. I bet you'd loosen up real nice."

My stomach twists. I try to glance past him towards the table, but he angles his body, blocking my way.

"I... I should check on Grace." My voice wavers, but I lift my chin, trying to look professional. Calm. Not like my heart is pounding with fear.

He lowers his voice, eyes raking over me in a way that makes my skin crawl. "I'd make it worth your while. Come on. Just one drink."

I freeze. My chest constricts.

And then... he's gone.

Yanked backwards so fast that he almost tumbles to the ground. A wall of muscle and fury steps between us.

Jack.

My whole body trembles as he looms in front of me, broad shoulders blocking out the room, his voice a growl that rattles my bones. "You think cornering women makes you a man? Get the fuck out of here, Ryan. Now."

Ryan gapes, color draining from his face. "I was just..."

"You were being a creep," Jack snaps. "And if you're not on your best behavior tomorrow, you'll be out of that wedding before you can blink. Am I fucking clear?"

Ryan mutters something under his breath, but the steel in Jack's glare has him backing away fast, his walk of shame dragging every eye in the room towards us.

And suddenly, all that attention lands squarely on me.

My cheeks burn. Embarrassment squeezes my throat. Before anyone can say anything, I bolt past the table, down the hall, fumbling for the first door I can find.

I lock it behind me, my chest heaving, tears stinging my eyes. The safety of the single-occupant bathroom won't last long, but at least it's something.

I lean back against the counter, pressing my hands over my face as the tears start to flow. My body shakes with humiliation and fear.

And then I feel it. A damp heat spreading across the bodice of my dress, and the telltale sting of letdown.

"Perfect," I whisper bitterly, blinking back tears. "Just perfect."

I grab some toilet paper and dab uselessly at the fabric, but there's no hiding the dark stains that are spreading across it. Not only did I cause a scene at the rehearsal dinner, but now I'm leaking like a damn faucet.

My boss is going to hear about this. I'm going to get fired. My career is going to be over before it's even begun. And I can't walk back out there, not like this. Everyone will see exactly what I've been hiding.

Tears blur my vision as I grip the sink. "Why now?" I choke; half a sob, half a curse.

A knock rattles the door. I jump, panic clawing at my throat.

"Occupied!" My voice comes out too high, too shaky, thick with the tears I'm trying to hold back.

There's silence for a moment, and then a voice I know instantly even though I've only heard it a few times. Deep, steady, commanding.

"Jenna. It's me."

Jack.

My knees weaken.

"I can hear you crying," he says softly, but there's an edge of steel under the gentleness. "Let me in."

"I... I can't."

"Jenna." My name is a growl, somehow rough and tender all at once. "Open the door. Now."

And I do. Because if anyone is going to see me like this, I'd rather it be him in private than an entire room full of people.

The door swings open, and he steps inside, filling the tiny space with his presence. He shuts it behind him, locking us in together, and then his eyes drop down to my dress.

Shock flickers across his face, but his voice is gentle. "First things first... are you okay? After what that asshole did?"

I swallow hard, ashamed. "I'm fine. Just... shaken. I think I've ruined everything."

"You didn't ruin a damn thing," he growls. "He did. You hear me? Ryan made a fool of himself. Not you. And it's Ryan that Grace and Aaron are mad at right now."

The conviction in his tone makes my chest ache. But when his gaze drifts lower, settling on the soaked fabric clinging to my breasts, humiliation surges all over again.

Embarrassment makes me blurt the words out before I can stop myself. "I'm lactating. It started when my brother and his husband adopted a baby girl. They worried she wouldn't thrive, so I... I induced, so I could donate my milk to them. I know it's strange. I know it's wrong, but..."

"Wrong?" His voice is sharp, incredulous. His eyes snap up to mine, blazing with something that makes my thighs clench. Hunger. Pure, unfiltered hunger. "It's beautiful and selfless that you would do this for your niece. It's not even close to being wrong."

I can hardly breathe as he steps closer, his body heat surrounding me. I had expected disgust, but all I see is need. Even more than before. As if this is the missing piece he didn't know he was searching for.

"Does your niece still need the milk?" His voice is low, almost reverent.

I shake my head, shame heating my cheeks once more. "She hasn't needed it for the last few months."

His lips curve into a dark, satisfied smile. "Good. Then your milk is all for me now."

My breath hitches, my whole body trembling as his hand rises slowly and deliberately to catch the edge of my bodice.

"Jack…"

"Shhh," he murmurs softly. "Let me take care of you."

And as he gently peels the top of my dress down, baring me inch by inch to his gaze, my shame dissolves into raw, aching anticipation.

I've never wanted anything so badly in my life.

Chapter Three

Jack

The scent hits me first.

Warm, sweet, rich. Like nothing I've ever known and everything I've ever needed. It fills the tiny bathroom, winding around me until I can barely breathe for the ache of it. My cock throbs, my chest pounds, and I know in my gut I'll never get enough.

Then I see her.

As I pull her dress lower, her breasts spill free. Heavy and round, her dusky pink nipples peaked and tight, with droplets of milk beading on each of them. Her cheeks are blotchy from crying, her lips trembling, her eyes wide and shining as if she expects me to recoil.

Recoil?

I want to drop to my fucking knees.

She's dripping with life, with nourishment, with a sweetness meant for me alone. My body responds like it's been starving all these years, just waiting for her. My mouth waters. My palms itch. Every primitive, feral instinct inside me screams to take, to claim, to drink until I'm full and then still demand more.

"Christ, Jenna..." My voice comes out raw, reverent, nearly shaking with the force of what's tearing through me. "Do you have any idea what you're doing to me right now?"

I step closer, drawn in like gravity, and the scent grows stronger, wrapping chains around my sanity.

"I didn't think you would want me when you found out about this," she says, her voice little more than a breathless whisper.

I reach up and gently cup one heavy tit in my hand, the skin slick with her leaking cream. "All this sweetness, and you thought no man would want it? You thought wrong, babygirl. I want it all."

She gasps softly. I have no idea if it's from my words or my touch, but I need the desperate little sounds she makes more than I need air right now.

My thumb traces a slow circle around her nipple. I watch in awe as the bead of milk quivers, and then trickles down.

"You've been full for so long, haven't you?" I murmur, leaning in closer. "Needing someone to drain you dry. To relieve all this pressure and make you feel good."

She shudders, eyes falling closed, her breath catching on a whimper. "Yes."

My cock is a rod of iron in my pants, throbbing so hard it hurts. My voice comes out harsh with barely restrained lust. "Then let me, babygirl. Let me give you what you need."

I don't give her a chance to respond before I lift her up to sit on the edge of the counter and my mouth closes over her nipple. She moans softly, one of her hands moving to the back of my head as I draw the sensitive nub between my lips. The first taste is a shock of electricity straight to my spine. A groan tears out of me as the warm, creamy liquid hits my tongue, and I suckle harder, demanding more.

I don't just want it. I fucking need it.

Her milk is rich and sweet and so goddamn pure it makes my dick throb. My whole body thrums with every pull of my mouth. I can already feel her relax, sinking deeper into the bliss of my touch, and a primal surge of satisfaction rises in me.

Mine. She's mine.

"Oh, God…" Jenna whimpers. She's gripping the back of my head so tightly I can feel the sting of her fingernails against my scalp. But I love it. I want her to mark me up. To brand me, scar me, leave no question that we are meant to be together.

I growl around her nipple, lapping the droplets from her soft, silky skin. The sound is muffled, greedy, desperate.

Her fingers twist in my hair. "Please. Don't stop."

My cock surges, pulsing against the zipper of my slacks, but the need to taste her is too strong to deny. So I switch to her other nipple, flicking the taut peak with my tongue.

She whimpers again, arching her back and offering her creamy tit. And I drink. I draw her deep into my mouth, and she writhes on the countertop, panting, whimpering, her legs parting and squeezing around my hips.

She's dripping, the musky scent of her arousal mingling with the rich sweetness of her milk. My cock aches, the tip leaking as precum beads. My balls are drawn up tight, and the urge to plunge inside her is overwhelming.

God, she'd look perfect with her belly round, her tits leaking just like this, our baby growing inside her.

Fuck. Where did that come from?

But I can't shake the thought. It burrows into my brain, making itself at home, until I'm dizzy with the need to make it real.

To put my seed in her, again and again and again, until it takes root.

The thought sends another pulse of precum into my boxers, and my cock strains for release. But I can't do that here. She deserves better than a quick fuck in a tiny restaurant bathroom. She deserves to be worshipped and spoiled and fucked like the fertile goddess that she is.

But I can give her relief, at least.

I slide a hand between her thighs, cupping her pussy through the lace of her panties. The material is soaked, clinging to her folds, and I groan against her breast. "Is this for me, babygirl? Does feeding me with your tits make your pussy wet and needy?"

"Yes," she moans. Her nails dig into the back of my neck, urging me closer.

"Mmm," I murmur, sucking on her nipple as I rub her pussy through the panties. Her clit is swollen and desperate for my touch, and I'm drunk on the knowledge that her body craves mine just as much as I crave hers.

I slide two fingers past the sodden fabric, tracing the seam of her lips until she shudders. Then I press them inside, groaning at the feel of her pussy clamping around me.

Fuck.

I've never felt anything so perfect.

She whimpers, arching her hips to take my fingers deeper. I thrust, crooking them inside her as her inner walls flutter and clench. I find a rhythm, thrusting with my fingers and sucking on her breast. Her body arches and trembles, and soon she's coming, her cries ringing off the walls as she gushes over my hand.

She's perfect. Absolutely perfect.

When she's finally trembling and spent, her tits fully drained, I force myself to ease back. My lips are wet, my throat still working around the taste of her, my body half-wild with the need to keep going.

But she's shaking, flushed, overwhelmed, and she's mine to care for. Not just to devour.

"Easy, babygirl," I murmur, helping her tug the bodice of her dress back into place. She won't meet my eyes, but I tilt her chin up until she does. "No shame. Not with me. Never with me."

Her lashes flutter as I shrug out of my jacket and settle it around her shoulders, broad enough to hide every damp patch. She looks small in it. Small and breakable and fucking beautiful.

"I'm taking you home," I tell her, voice rough with need. "I'll get you bathed, cleaned up, taken care of. And then I can claim your pretty little cunt properly."

Panic sparks across her face. She shakes her head quickly. "I... I can't. If I leave now, it'll look bad. I'll get in trouble with my boss. But I can't go back out there when I'm such a mess either. What am I going to do, Jack?"

I grit my teeth, every instinct screaming at me to scoop her up in my arms and take her home anyway, but I force myself to relent. No matter how much I want her, I'm not going to do anything that might risk her job.

"Okay, here's what we'll do, Jenna. You go home, and I'll stay here to cover for you. I'll tell Grace you had to leave, that you were upset after what that bastard pulled, which isn't even a lie, really. She won't think less of you."

Relief softens her expression, and I press my hand to the small of her back, guiding her quietly through the corridors and out into the night air.

"Thank you for everything you've done for me tonight," she says, glancing up at me with a soft smile teasing the corners of her lips.

"No need to thank me, babygirl. For any of it. I will always take care of what's mine."

Her breath catches, and she pauses for a moment before continuing the short walk to her car. She fumbles for her keys, and before she can escape me entirely, I catch her wrist.

"I can't let you go without this," I rasp.

And then I kiss her.

It's not soft. It's not tentative. It's hunger and promise and possession, her sweet little gasp swallowed into my mouth as I claim her pretty lips for the first time. She wraps her arms around my neck as she kisses me back, swaying into me, and I nearly lose the battle with myself right there. But I let her go because I have to. For now.

"Tomorrow," I promise against her lips. "I'll see you tomorrow, Jenna."

She nods, dazed, before slipping into her car and driving away, my jacket still drowning her frame.

I watch until her taillights vanish, then turn back towards the restaurant, jaw clenched.

Grace is waiting for me when I return to the table, worry clouding her face. "Dad? Did you find Jenna? Where is she?"

"She was shaken up after what happened with Ryan," I tell her smoothly. "She needed to go home, but she'll be at the wedding tomorrow to take care of everything."

Grace's mouth tightens. "I still can't believe he acted like such a jerk. His behavior was completely unacceptable."

Aaron grimaces, running a hand through his hair. "I'll talk to him tonight. Make sure he keeps his distance from her tomorrow."

"See that you do," I bite out.

The night goes on, but I'm barely present. My daughter and her fiancé chatter, wine flows, laughter swells again.

But I can't bring myself to eat or drink anything else. Because I don't want to lose the taste of Jenna.

She's still sweet and warm on my tongue, clinging to my lips, flooding every thought until I'm aching with the need to have her back in my arms.

She's mine now. And no force on earth is going to take her from me.

Chapter Four

♥

Jenna

The vineyard is buzzing.

The air smells like roses and fresh-cut grass; the sun is high and warm, and I'm moving through it all with my clipboard in one hand and my headset clipped firmly in place.

I'm in wedding-planner mode. Locked in. Efficient. Focused.

Mostly.

"Bride's family to the left, and the groom's to the right," I coach one of the groomsmen as the first guests begin to arrive. He nods, straightening his tie as he heads off to usher people to their seats.

I do a quick visual scan of the ceremony space. Arches are draped with pale pink flowers, and the chairs are lined in perfect rows with linen bows fluttering in the breeze. Everything is exactly how I designed it. Exactly how Grace asked for it.

A smile tugs at my lips.

I did this. All of it.

I've been dreaming of running my own events for years, and today is my first real solo wedding under the company banner. No manager breathing down my neck, no senior planner second-guessing me. Just me, and everything is running like a dream.

I make my way towards the main house, offering warm smiles and gentle nudges to guests who arrive looking a little confused. I check my phone. The hair and makeup team should be finishing up soon. Time to check on the bride.

Before I make it there, I spot Aaron pacing near the groom's suite, nervously smoothing his jacket sleeves.

I approach quietly. "Everything okay?"

He startles slightly, then laughs under his breath. "Yeah. I think so. Just... wedding day jitters, you know? I really want Grace to be happy today."

I nod. "That's completely normal. If you weren't nervous, I'd be worried. But you've got this, okay? Grace adores you. She's practically floating this morning."

His shoulders relax, tension easing from his face. "Thanks, Jenna. Honestly, you've made all of this so easy. I don't know how you do it."

I flash a quick smile. "That's a trade secret. If I told you, then I'd have to kill you."

He laughs and heads back inside, and I turn towards the bridal suite. But as I walk, the buzzing energy in my chest shifts. It's not nerves. Not excitement.

It's the knowledge that I'll be seeing Jack soon.

I haven't seen him since last night when he pulled me from the most embarrassing moment of my life, peeled down my dress and fed from my leaking breasts like he couldn't get enough... then kissed me like he already owned me.

My body reacts just from thinking about it.

A pulse of heat flares low in my belly. My breasts throb behind the boning of my dress, full and heavy again even though I pumped everything I had before leaving the house this morning. It's too soon, but my body doesn't seem to care. It's as if he triggered something in me that I can't shut off.

Focus, Jenna. This is Grace's day. Not yours.

I square my shoulders, grip my clipboard tighter, and head towards the bridal suite with brisk, determined steps.

The suite hums with energy the moment I slip inside. Grace is perched in a chair by the window, glowing in a robe as two of her bridesmaids fuss over her. The makeup artist leans in close, dusting shimmer across Grace's cheekbones, while the hairstylist carefully pins the last curls into place.

It's a happy chaos, with laughter and music playing softly from someone's phone. The faint scent of hairspray and roses fills the air.

"Jenna!" Grace beams at me in the mirror, her eyes bright. "Tell me everything's on track out there."

"Everything is perfect," I assure her. "The florals arrived on time, the chairs are set, and guests are already being seated. The ceremony is going to be stunning."

She exhales in relief, her smile widening. "Of course it is. You've been amazing through all of this."

I smile, but guilt pricks sharply in my chest. If Grace knew what I'd done with her father last night, I doubt she would be so complimentary.

I check in briefly with the hairstylist, nodding approval at the polished updos, then glance at the makeup artist's work. Everything looks flawless. I murmur encouragements, smoothing nerves where I can, hiding the fact that I'm barely keeping my own in check.

And then the air shifts.

The door opens, and a new presence fills the suite.

Jack Westmore.

He stands framed in the doorway, tall and broad, tuxedo fitting him like it was made for him alone. The chatter around the room dips for a moment, the bridesmaids straightening instinctively. My heart stops for a brief second before it starts slamming against my ribs.

Memories hit me like a tidal wave. His mouth on my breasts, the rough velvet of his tongue, his fingers inside me until I shattered, the way he kissed me like he'd never let me go. My body reacts instantly, a rush of heat between my thighs, a heavy ache in my chest.

"Dad!" Grace lights up, jumping from her chair to hug him. "You look so handsome."

"You look beautiful, sweetheart," Jack says warmly, kissing her cheek before turning his attention to the rest of us.

And then his gaze lands on me.

I can't move.

"Jenna's made everything so beautiful," Grace gushes, tugging him a little closer. "I don't know what I would have done without her."

Jack's eyes never leave mine as he replies, his voice smooth, low. "Jenna does have an exquisite taste."

The bridesmaids murmur agreement, thinking he means the flowers, the colors, the decor. Grace grins at him, pleased.

But I know better.

I see it in the heat of his gaze, in the way his eyes linger far too long on my lips before dragging slowly down my body. He isn't talking about the wedding. He's talking about me. About last night. About the milk he tasted from my breasts like he was starving for it.

My breath stutters. My cheeks flame.

Grace is standing right there. Her bridesmaids too. But I can't look away from him. The electricity crackles between us, undeniable, dangerous.

And the guilt slices sharper than ever, because no matter how wrong it is, my body is screaming the truth.

I want him.

Grace steps back from her father and smooths her robe over her hips, her smile radiant with anticipation.

"Okay," she says, clapping her hands softly. "Time to get dressed."

The bridesmaids buzz to life again, laughter and excitement spilling into the room as they gather around the garment bag hanging from the full-length mirror in the corner. I nod, tucking my clipboard against my chest and moving towards the door.

"I'll give you all a few minutes," I say, my voice calmer than I feel. "I'll be right outside if you need anything."

Grace beams at me. Jack tells his daughter that he'll be right outside with me, waiting for her to be ready so he can walk her down the aisle. As he follows me out of the suite, I feel his eyes on me, and every inch of my skin burns under his gaze.

Once we're in the hallway, Jack leans against the far wall, arms folded across his chest, tux perfectly tailored, his expression unreadable. But his eyes... oh God, those eyes. They rake over me like I'm something he wants to unwrap and devour.

I clutch my clipboard tighter, trying not to shake.

"Have you seen Ryan yet today?" he asks, his voice tight.

The question surprises me, but I shake my head. "Not yet. I assume he's been in the groom's suite with Aaron."

He nods. "Okay. I just wanted to make sure he was behaving himself. I don't want him touching what's mine."

Mine.

His voice rumbles over the word, low and possessive, and my core clenches. My nipples are hard, pressing against my dress, and I can't stop myself from remembering how his mouth felt on them, hot and greedy.

How his hands felt on my thighs, strong and confident.

How his fingers felt inside me, thick and skilled, taking me apart in a matter of seconds.

The silence stretches, the air around us brimming with tension. I should leave. I should go check something. Anything. But I don't move. Neither does he.

His gaze drops down to my chest, lingers. His eyes darken, and for one dizzy second, I think he might reach for me. I want him to.

But he doesn't move. There's too much risk. Too many doors nearby. Too many people who could walk past.

His voice drops even lower. "Later. I need to taste you again, baby-girl. It's all I can fucking think about."

I'm trembling now, my knees threatening to give way. My nipples throb, aching to be suckled, and there's no doubt in my mind that he knows exactly what he's doing to me.

He pushes away from the wall, adjusting his jacket sleeves. He's close enough that I can smell his aftershave, and I nearly melt into a puddle on the floor.

"Later," he says again, voice rough. "I'll find you."

"Okay," I whisper.

His jaw tightens, and for a moment, he looks almost pained. But then the door to the bridal suite opens, and he steps back, putting some distance between us.

The makeup artist and hairstylist slip out, giving me a warm smile as they pass between us, shattering the moment.

I take a deep breath, trying to get myself under control. I glance at the clipboard clutched in my hands. It's shaking slightly, and my mind feels fuzzy, overwhelmed.

Focus, Jenna.

I have a job to do. And I'm determined to do it well, even if the father of the bride is hell-bent on driving me wild.

***

The music swells, soft and romantic, carried on the breeze across the vineyard lawn.

I stand off to the side, half-hidden by a climbing rose trellis, watching everything unfold. But my heart is thudding too fast, and my legs feel shaky.

Because he's walking her down the aisle.

Jack Westmore, tall and commanding in his tux, his arm linked with Grace's as they move slowly between the rows of seated guests. He looks every inch the proud father, stoic and strong, a faint smile tugging at the corners of his mouth.

But his eyes...

His eyes find mine. Just for a second. Just long enough for heat to curl low in my belly and my breath to catch.

I look away. I have to.

Come on, Jenna, I think to myself. *Focus. You're here to do a job. You are not here to fall apart because the father of the bride makes your knees go weak with a single glance.*

Grace reaches the altar, beaming. Jack kisses her cheek, whispers something I can't hear, and steps aside.

Aaron's waiting for her, handsome in his tailored suit, eyes shining as he takes both of Grace's hands in his. The officiant welcomes everyone and begins the ceremony.

It's beautiful. Not even the sight of Ryan standing beside the groom could ruin this moment.

The vows are heartfelt. Grace's voice trembles when she talks about how Aaron has been her safe place since high school. He smiles as if he's the proudest man in the entire world.

The guests sniffle. Bridesmaids dab at their eyes. Cameras click softly in the background.

I should be listening. But all I can feel is the weight of Jack's gaze.

Every time I glance across the rows of guests to where he sits in the front row, he's watching me. Never looking away.

And I'm helpless against the way my body aches with the memory of his touch. I shift my weight, pressing my thighs together, trying to chase away the ache. But it only sharpens.

The officiant says, "Do you, Grace, take this man..." and I force myself to refocus.

Grace's voice is clear. "I do."

The words are repeated for the groom, and Aaron's voice is thick with emotion. "I do."

The officiant smiles. "Then, by the power vested in me..."

There's cheering before he even finishes the sentence. Grace and Aaron kiss beneath the floral arch, petals fluttering down around them. The guests erupt in applause.

It's perfect. Absolutely perfect.

I clap with everyone else, smiling through the sting in my eyes. Happy tears, mostly. A little pride.

And a lot of confusion.

Because as the newlyweds turn to face their guests, hand in hand, glowing with joy... my gaze finds Jack's again.

And the way he looks at me makes me forget how to breathe.

Chapter Five

Jenna

Grace and Aaron are wrapped up in each other, swaying in the middle of the dance floor like there's no one else in the world.

It's their first dance as husband and wife, and it's everything I imagined it would be. Slow, tender, and romantic. The kind of moment they will remember for the rest of their lives.

I stand at the edge of the room, fingers laced together in front of me while I sway a little myself in time with the ballad that the band is playing.

Everything has gone perfectly. Not a single delay or hiccup. The catering team I hired turned up on time, the food was flawless, and the table decorations had been stunning.

Even Ryan, the best man, has been shockingly well-behaved. Not a leer, not a comment, not even a passing glance in my direction all day.

I should be proud. Relieved. Euphoric, even.

But I'm not. Because the only thing I can think about is Jack.

All day long, I've felt him watching me. Across the vineyard during the ceremony. From his place at the head table during dinner. Silent and hungry, like he's barely leashed.

And I've been waiting.

Waiting for the moment he'd take me aside like he said he would. For him to touch me again. To feed from me the way he did last night, when he'd treated me like I was the only one in the world who could satisfy him.

The ache has been building since morning, low and slow and punishing. My breasts feel heavy, sensitive, the tight bodice of my dress doing nothing to ease the pressure. I'm full. So full that I'm growing desperate for relief.

I know he'll come. He has to. And when he does, I'll give him anything. Everything.

The song ends, and the newlyweds laugh as the crowd erupts in applause. The dance floor starts to fill with guests. Glasses clink. Music swells again.

And then I feel a presence at my back.

I don't have to look to know it's him.

Jack's hand brushes mine. Barely a touch, but it sends a bolt of heat through me so fast that I nearly gasp.

"Come with me," he murmurs, his voice a rumble in my ear.

I follow him without hesitation.

He leads me through the rear doors of the reception hall, down a short hallway lined with stone, and into a cool, dimly lit cellar tucked beneath the venue.

Wine barrels line the walls, the air thick with oak and something sweet and dark and earthy.

And we're all alone.

I barely have time to turn to face him before my back hits the nearest wall, the exposed brickwork cool against the skin on my back left exposed by my dress. His mouth crashes into mine, hot and possessive, and his hands are already tugging frantically at the top half of my dress.

I help him, reaching behind me for the zipper, and between the two of us, we have it loosened and peeled down to my waist in seconds. My breasts spring free, heavy and aching, and his mouth falls to them with a groan.

My head falls back, eyes closing. I whimper as his tongue swirls, and then moan as his teeth graze my nipples.

"I couldn't fucking wait any longer," he mutters, taking a nipple deep into his mouth and sucking hard. The pressure builds painfully behind my nipple for a moment, before the sweet relief of my letdown hits.

He grunts as the milk floods his mouth, and the sensation is so intense that it makes my knees weak. He's not even touching me between my legs, but the pleasure is already so good I think I might come from the sensation.

"Jack," I gasp, clinging to his shoulders.

He growls and wraps one hand around my breast, squeezing, massaging, coaxing more milk from my aching nipple.

"Give it to me," he mutters, his lips brushing against my dripping nipple, and then his mouth is on me again, feeding greedily.

He's rough this time. Desperate. It's nothing like last night, when he savored every drop. No, this is raw need. A craving that he's barely holding onto.

He moves to my other breast, taking it deep in his mouth and sucking, groaning.

"Oh God," I whimper, bringing my hands to the back of his head, my fingers running through his hair as I hold him against my breast. "That feels so good, Jack. I've been needing this so badly all day."

He pulls his mouth from my nipple with something that sounds like a pained groan, and he brings his lips to mine. He tastes sweet and nutty, the taste of my milk coating his lips and tongue as he kisses me hard, deep, making me whimper.

"I've been needing it too, babygirl. Needing to fill my belly with your sweet cream," he rasps. "It's the only thing I can think about. How it's going to feel when I drink from you again."

I don't know why it drives me so crazy when he says things like that, but it does. My pussy is slick and aching, and I know the fabric of my underwear is probably soaked.

"And this milk is all mine, Jenna. I'm not going to share until my baby is here, taking all the nourishment they need from your gorgeous tits. But you'll still need to feed me too, babygirl. I don't think I'll ever be able to get enough of you."

His mouth latches back onto a nipple, and it takes me a moment to process his words through the haze of pleasure fogging my brain.

"Baby?" I ask, the word turning to a moan as he nips at the stiff peak in his mouth with his teeth.

"Damn right," he growls, sliding a hand up to rest on my flat stomach. "I can't wait to see you full and round. Watch these pretty tits swell and fill with even more milk. Watch my baby grow inside you."

I moan, the thought almost too much. It's filthy. And it's way too soon to be talking about babies.

But it's the hottest damn thing anyone has ever said to me.

His words have an effect on him too. He's hard, his erection pressing insistently into my hip. I'm so tempted to reach down and stroke him, to feel his thickness in my hand. But he's focused entirely on my breasts. He's kneading them roughly, sucking and licking and biting like he's ravenous for it. Like he can't get enough.

And I love it. The sensation is intense, the ache giving way to pleasure so strong I'm afraid I'm going to lose my mind.

"You're mine, Jenna," he says, his voice ragged. "And when I claim your needy little pussy with my seed, I'll make you come so fucking hard you won't ever want anyone but me. You'll forget all about your ex-boyfriends, too. You'll know that your cunt, and your womb, are mine. All fucking mine."

Oh, God.

I can't believe he's saying all of this, and I can't believe how much I want it. He's so dominant, and possessive, and demanding. And I crave it all.

"I am all yours, Jack. Nobody else has ever... ever been inside me."

My face flushes with embarrassment at my confession, but I need to tell him. I need to let him know that he's going to be my first. That I belong entirely to him.

"You're a virgin?" he asks, his tone incredulous, but the look in his eyes is pure, hungry lust. "Fuck, babygirl. I can't wait to get my cock in that tight little cunt. You'll be so snug and wet for me, won't you? Going to squeeze me so good. Going to take every drop of cum from my balls and keep it all safe in your womb, won't you?"

"Yes," I pant, and God, if he keeps talking like that, I might actually come just from his words.

"That's right," he growls. "Gonna pump you full. Get you so full of my cum that you're dripping. And then I'm going to plug you and keep every single drop where it belongs. Where it will take root and grow."

"Now?" I ask, the word slipping out before I can stop it.

Jack lets out a low groan. "I want to, babygirl. Fuck, I want that so badly. But when I breed you, I want to be able to take my time. I want you spread out and bare and begging for me. Begging me to put a baby in you. I'm going to stretch your virgin pussy with my cock, and then I'm going to flood your fertile little womb with my seed. Something like that deserves to happen when we have time and privacy. Not a quickie in a wine cellar."

I let out a whining sound. Disappointment, arousal, frustration. They're all mingling together in my body, making me ache so much that I can barely stand it.

Jack chuckles, the sound warm and low, and then he's kissing me again, slow and deep and sweet.

"But you're in luck," he murmurs against my mouth, his voice rough. "There are plenty of things we can do in the meantime. And right now, there's something I need you to do for me, babygirl."

"What is it?"

"I need you to sit on the barrel over there and spread those gorgeous thighs for me."

I look around, noticing the small barrel a few feet away. I'm not sure what he has planned, but the idea of it makes my whole body tingle.

He helps me off the wall, supporting me as I wobble a little. My breasts are still bare, and the cool air feels good on my heated skin.

"Sit," he instructs, guiding me towards the barrel.

I do, and he kneels in front of me, his hands sliding up my thighs. His touch makes me shiver, and when his hands push the skirt of my dress up, my breath hitches.

He hooks his fingers around the sides of my thong and drags it down. I lift myself slightly, helping him, and when the scrap of lace has been pulled all the way down, I'm left completely bare.

His eyes remain locked on mine as he folds the fabric and slips it into the pocket of his tux.

"This is mine now," he says.

"Yes," I say simply. My voice is soft and shaky.

Jack's gaze drifts lower, down to my bare mound, and he lets out a groan. "Fuck, Jenna. You have the prettiest pussy. It's practically begging for my mouth. My cock. Fuck, I can't wait to sink inside you and make you mine."

He's barely touched me, and yet I'm trembling. He's staring at my most intimate place like he's mesmerized, and the hunger in his eyes makes the ache between my legs that much more intense.

"Please," I whimper.

Jack's lips quirk in a smile, and he leans closer, his breath ghosting over my sensitive flesh.

"Don't worry, babygirl. I'm going to take care of you. Give you everything you need."

He presses a soft kiss against the top of my thigh, and I shiver. He does the same thing on the other side, and then he's moving closer and closer, until I can feel his breath against my center.

And then he's licking me, one long stroke from the bottom of my entrance all the way up, ending at the swollen nub above.

I cry out, the sensation so intense. My whole body jolts, and I grip the edges of the barrel.

Jack holds me open, his thumbs tracing the crease where my thighs meet my hips, and then his mouth is back, his tongue delving deep. He licks and sucks, his moans muffled as he devours me.

"Jack," I whimper, arching my back and grinding my pussy against his mouth. "Please."

He slides two fingers inside me, stretching my entrance, and I let out a long moan.

"That's right, babygirl. Let me hear you. Let me hear how good it feels."

His tongue flicks across my clit, and I nearly scream. The pleasure is so sharp, so intense, that it's almost painful.

"Oh, God. Yes, Jack, yes!"

His fingers pump in and out of my soaking wet channel, the rhythmic squelching sounds echoing through the cellar. He adds a third finger, stretching me even more, and the pressure is so perfect that it's driving me wild.

I'm rocking against his hand, meeting every thrust, and the orgasm building inside me is unlike anything I've ever felt. It's all-consuming, like a tidal wave looming on the horizon.

Jack curls his fingers, pressing up into the front wall of my channel, and his mouth closes around my clit, suckling the sensitive bundle of nerves with as much enthusiasm as he sucked the milk from my breasts.

The orgasm crashes into me. I shatter, crying out as waves of pleasure wash over me. Jack keeps sucking and thrusting his fingers, drawing out every second of bliss until I'm completely spent.

He presses a final kiss to the top of my mound, and then slowly withdraws his fingers, leaving me empty and throbbing.

"Good girl," he whispers. "You're so beautiful when you come, Jenna. Fucking breathtaking."

He rises, his mouth crashing into mine, and his hands roam all over my body, like he can't decide where he wants to touch me first.

His jacket is still on, his shirt perfectly pressed and tucked into his pants. He looks so composed, so elegant. And I'm a wreck. My dress is loose and gaping at the front, breasts bare and nipples red and raw. My pussy is wet and swollen, and my knees are trembling so hard that I can barely stay upright.

He doesn't seem to mind, though. His cock is hard and straining against his pants, and I can't resist reaching out, cupping the hard length through the material.

"Do you want me to...? I mean, can I...?"

I can't bring myself to say the words, but that doesn't stop me craving to please him as much as he's pleased me the last two evenings. He captures my wrist though, pulling my hand away with a groan.

"As much as I want that, babygirl, I'm not wasting my seed like that. It's all going inside you when I take you home after the wedding is over. We'll have the whole night, and all day tomorrow. And every night after that."

He says it with such certainty, like it's a given. Like he already knows that this will never end.

And I want that too. More than I've ever wanted anything in my life.

Chapter Six

Jenna

Jack helps me sit up gently, his hands slow and careful as he pulls the straps of my dress back over my shoulders. His fingers linger against my skin, warm and reverent, like he can't quite bear to stop touching me.

I'm still shaking from the orgasm. My lips are swollen. My thighs are slick.

And my heart is a complete mess.

He adjusts the fabric, making sure it sits just right, then brushes a few strands of hair back from my face. His touch is tender, making my chest ache in a way that has nothing to do with milk.

Then he leans in, pressing a soft kiss to my lips.

"I have to go back," he murmurs, his forehead resting against mine. "Can't have the bride wondering where her father disappeared to."

I let out a shaky laugh, still breathless. "Right. That might be awkward."

His hand trails down my arm. "But don't think for one second that we're done, babygirl."

My breath hitches.

"When this reception is over," he says, voice low and full of promise, "I'm taking you home with me. I'm going to strip you bare. Spread you open. And make you mine in every way that counts."

Heat floods my cheeks. My legs. My core. I can't speak. I just nod, eyes wide, completely undone all over again.

He presses one last lingering kiss to my cheek, then turns and slips out of the cellar, his footsteps fading into the distance.

I stay where I am for a minute longer, swaying slightly, trying to collect myself. My whole body feels like it's still vibrating from the way he touched me. Licked me. Praised me.

God, what am I doing?

I straighten my dress, smooth down my skirt, and gather what's left of my dignity. It takes everything I have just to make my legs move towards the exit.

But when I push open the door, I walk right into Ryan.

"Oh," I gasp, stepping back instinctively.

He looks down at me with a smug little smirk, with a wine glass in one hand.

"Funny," he says, eyes narrowing. "Didn't I just see Jack Westmore come out of here a minute ago?"

My stomach twists.

"I... I don't know what you're talking about."

"Sure you don't." He lifts his glass to his lips and takes a slow sip, his eyes never leaving mine. "So what were you two doing in the cellar, sweetheart? Checking on the wine?"

I try to move past him. "Please let me through."

But he steps in front of me again, body angled just enough to block the hallway. Not touching me. But too close. Too smug.

"It must have been quite a tasting," he says with a pointed look down my body. "Did you give him a sample of something special?"

My face burns. "Leave me alone."

"I'm just saying," he continues, his tone maddeningly casual, "if Grace finds out you were messing around with her father during her wedding, she's not going to be thrilled."

"Stop."

"And when she tells your boss what happened? Oof." He grins. "Hope you've got a backup plan, sweetheart. You'll be out of a job before you have time to pack up your little clipboard."

Panic hits me full force.

I shake my head, swallowing hard. "Please... don't do this."

"Oh, I'm not going to do anything. As long as you do the smart thing." He leans in just slightly, voice dropping. "Tell Jack it's over. Tell him you're not interested. And then we can all move on with our lives."

I stare at him, heart pounding in my ears.

"Fine," I whisper. "I'll tell him."

Ryan straightens, smug satisfaction radiating from him. He nods once, like a man who thinks he's just won something.

And I barge past him, my shoulders shaking and my throat tight.

The corridor blurs as I walk quickly, needing to get away from his eyes, his voice, his stupid smug face. The sound of laughter and music filters through the walls, but none of it feels real.

All I can hear is the voice echoing in my head.

You'll be out of a job before you have time to pack up your little clipboard.

God, I can't lose this job. Not after everything I've worked for. Not after how hard I fought to prove I could do this.

But Jack...

My steps falter, and I brace a hand on the wall, sucking in a breath.

I want him. I want him so badly it hurts. He makes me feel more seen, more wanted, more accepted than anyone ever has. And the way he touches me, the way he drinks from me...

It's not just heat. It's not just lust.

It's *connection*.

And now I have to throw it all away.

I wipe my face and steel myself. I can do this. I need to just get it over with quickly. Like ripping off a band-aid.

When I step back into the reception hall, it feels louder than before. Guests are dancing. Champagne is flowing. Fairy lights twinkle across the ceiling, and everything looks like a dream.

And Jack is standing just to the side of the dance floor, his eyes scanning the crowd.

When his gaze lands on mine, something in his face softens. He straightens, his whole body tightening like he's preparing to come to me.

I cut across the room before he can move. I need to do this quickly. Cleanly.

He opens his mouth to speak, but I get there first. My voice is quiet. Barely audible over the music.

"I can't see you again."

Jack stills. His jaw ticks. "Excuse me?"

I swallow, avoiding his eyes. "It's over."

"No." The word is a growl, sharp and instant. "No, that's not what you were saying five minutes ago. Not after the way you..." He cuts himself off, breath heavy. "Tell me why, Jenna. What made you change your mind about us so quickly?"

I look over his shoulder. Ryan's there, leaning against the bar, watching us like a hawk. Jack's gaze follows mine.

My hands shake. "He threatened to tell Grace if I didn't end things with you. Said she'd be bound to go to my boss and complain about me fooling around with her father on her wedding day. And then I'd lose my job." My voice cracks on the final word, and tears sting my eyes.

Jack's expression changes in a heartbeat. The fire in his eyes is immediate and brutal.

He doesn't say anything at first, though. He just steps forward, cups the back of my head, and presses a kiss to my forehead.

"I'll handle it," he murmurs. "Don't worry, babygirl. I'm not going to let that fucker take you away from me."

And then he turns and walks away.

I don't move. I just watch as he weaves through the crowd, heading straight for Grace.

My stomach twists so hard I think I might be sick. I wonder if I should follow him, give her my side of the story, but I'm frozen in place.

I can't hear what he's saying to her. I can only see her face; how she frowns, then blinks. Her mouth moves, her brows pull together with confusion.

Then her expression shifts from one of shock to anger.

My knees go weak. She's going to be so mad at me. I've ruined everything. If I manage to keep my job after this, it will be a goddamn miracle.

Then Grace turns fast and storms across the reception hall like a hurricane in white satin, her veil floating behind her like a war banner.

But she's not moving towards me. It's Ryan who gets the full force of her wrath.

I watch in frozen horror as she rips into him without hesitation. With no concern about who's watching. Just pure fury. I still can't hear what's being said over the music, but her hands gesture wildly, and she shoves at his shoulder while she yells.

Grace points to the exit, and Ryan tries to argue, but she's not hearing it.

And then Jack is there too.

He grabs Ryan by the lapels and yanks him close, his mouth right at the other man's ear, and judging by the look of fury on Jack's face, I think I'm pleased I can't hear what's being said right now.

Ryan's eyes widen. Jack shoves him hard once, and he stumbles backwards before scurrying off like the coward he is. He's red-faced and seething, but he doesn't look back.

I barely have time to process what I just witnessed before Grace turns, her veil fluttering softly behind her, and makes her way back towards me with Jack beside her.

She's... smiling.

Not tight-lipped. Not forced. But warm and easy and full of affection.

I have no idea what's happening.

"Jenna," she says gently, her eyes kind. "I'm so sorry Ryan has been such a jerk this weekend. Aaron spoke to him after the meal last night, and he promised to be on his best behavior today. But apparently he didn't mean it."

My lips part, but nothing comes out.

"I'm really glad Dad told me what Ryan was trying to pull tonight," she continues. My gaze flicks to Jack, who stands silently beside her, his eyes locked intently on me.

"You've done such an incredible job today," Grace says, stepping forward to take my hands in hers. "This was everything I ever dreamed of. And honestly... if my dad is going to fall for someone, I'm glad it's someone as sweet and utterly lovely as you, Jenna."

I blink hard, but the tears still gather. I can't believe this is happening, but I'm not about to argue with her. "I... thank you. That means so much to me."

She gives my hands a squeeze. "Aaron and I are heading out now. Honeymoon time." Her grin is full of sparkle. "But I'll be sending a very generous tip later, along with glowing compliments to your boss. You've earned it all. And then some."

I laugh, breathless with relief. "Safe travels. You both deserve all the happiness in the world."

Grace pulls me into a hug, and then Jack leans in to press a kiss to her forehead. She hugs him too, and then she and Aaron are gone, sent off with a flurry of cheers, clinking glasses, and bubbles being blown into the night air.

The reception is still going on behind us, minus the bride and groom now. But here, in this quiet little corner... it's just us.

Just me and Jack.

He turns to me, his eyes heavy with heat and something deeper. And the second his fingers close around mine, the world steadies. My heart races. My pulse thrums in anticipation.

"It's time to take my girl home," he says, his voice low and full of promise. "Time to make her mine."

Chapter Seven

Jack

My hands fumble with the keys like I'm seventeen and two seconds from blowing my load in my pants. God knows I'm hard enough for that to happen. Jenna stands just behind me, close enough that I can hear her shallow breaths and the way she shifts her weight from one foot to the other on the porch.

She wants this. I can feel it in her.

And fuck, I'm going to give it to her.

The second the lock clicks, I slam the door open and turn to her, taking in those flushed cheeks and that eager sparkle in her eyes.

I can't wait another goddamn second, so I grab her.

She gasps softly, but her arms fly around my shoulders at the same time her legs hook around my waist, like her body already knows what to do. Her chest presses against mine, and her breath is quick and warm against my neck.

I hold her like I've done this a thousand times. Like she belongs in my arms, against me, wrapped around me like this.

I kick the door shut behind us, and then I start to climb.

One step at a time, slow and steady, because I want her to feel it. Every flex of my muscles. Every shift of her weight in my grip. Every inch she rises towards the place where I'm going to finally ruin her sweet, untouched little body.

Her fingers dig into my shoulders as I reach the top.

"You're mine now," I growl, lips brushing her ear. "And when I'm done with you tonight, your womb will know it too."

She shivers. Whimpers. Tightens her grip around me.

I shoulder the bedroom door open and carry her inside, towards the bed I've dreamed of laying her in since the moment I saw her.

Then I set her down gently, slowly, letting her slide down my body inch by torturous inch until her feet hit the floor. I step back just enough to look at her. My sweet, blushing, beautiful girl.

Her eyes are wide, her lips parted. She's waiting for me. Waiting for my next move.

My heart fucking aches.

"I can't take my eyes off you," I tell her, voice rough and low. "Not for one second. You're the most beautiful thing I've ever seen, babygirl. Do you have any idea what you do to me?"

She shakes her head, cheeks flushing.

"Everything," I say. "You make me feel everything. Desire. Need. Protectiveness. Like I could fucking kill anyone who even looked at you wrong. Like I want to possess every inch of you. Keep you all to myself."

Her chest rises and falls, the swell of her breasts visible above the neckline of her pretty dress.

I reach behind her, pulling the zipper down. "I need you, Jenna. And I'm not going to hold back tonight. Are you ready for that?"

"Yes," she breathes, the word shaky and desperate.

"Good." I pull the straps of her dress down, letting the material fall and pool at her feet.

My gaze roams over her naked body, and my cock pulses in my pants. After I stole her panties earlier, she's left in nothing but her heels now that her dress is gone, and fuck if it isn't the sexiest thing I've ever seen.

"So beautiful," I growl. "Every single inch."

"And you," she says, hands trembling slightly as she reaches up to push my suit jacket off my shoulders. "I want to see you too, Jack."

She doesn't hesitate as she unfastens my shirt, and I let her.

Let her take her time, revealing my chest slowly, like a present being unwrapped. Her hands are small and soft and reverent, and when she slides her fingers beneath the material, touching me with her bare skin, my pulse kicks hard.

Her hands are hesitant as they drop lower, and when she reaches the waistband of my pants, she looks up at me with a questioning look in her eyes.

"Go on," I whisper.

Her touch is feather-light as she undoes the buckle. The zipper.

Then she's pushing my pants and boxers down, and my cock springs free. It's heavy and thick and leaking, and the way her breath catches when she sees it makes me even harder.

"Oh," she whispers. "It's... you're..."

"Big."

"Yes." She licks her lips, her cheeks darkening. "So big."

She reaches out, tentatively wrapping her hand around me, and I have to hold back a string of curse words. Her soft skin feels so fucking good around my shaft, and when she gives an experimental stroke, it takes everything in me not to lose control right then and there.

"Fuck," I hiss. "That feels so damn good, babygirl."

In an attempt to distract myself from her touch so I don't embarrass myself, I grab a handful of her hair and pull her closer, crushing my mouth against hers.

Her lips are eager and pliant, parting for me instantly, and the way she melts into my kiss is intoxicating. It's messy. Hungry.

And when her tongue meets mine, sliding against me in the filthiest fucking dance, it sends a rush of heat straight to my balls.

I break the kiss, breathing hard, and press my lips to her temple instead.

"Get on the bed."

She doesn't hesitate. In fact, she scrambles to obey, crawling backwards onto the mattress. She keeps her eyes on me the whole time, a flush spreading across her chest and neck.

She's so beautiful, so goddamn perfect, and the sight of her spread out on my bed in nothing more than her heels is almost more than I can bear.

I reach down, wrapping my hand around my dick and giving it a slow stroke.

"Tell me what you want, Jenna. Let me hear you say it."

"I want you," she says, voice breathy.

"Be more specific. Where do you want me?"

She pauses. Bites her lip. Then she moves her hands down, fingers trailing over her collarbone. Across her tits, teasing her nipples until they harden into stiff peaks. Over the soft curve of her stomach, and lower still, until she reaches the apex of her thighs.

Holy shit.

I watch in complete awe as she opens herself for me, showing me the most intimate part of her body. Her fingers are soft and slow as they explore her folds, and when they finally slide inside, she lets out a soft moan.

"I want you here, Jack. Inside me. And I want you to fill me with your cum. I want it all inside me so it can take root and grow. So that it'll become a baby. Our baby."

I've never moved so fast in my life.

Before I can even blink, I've kicked off my shoes and pants and boxers and grabbed her wrist, roughly pulling her hand away from what's mine.

Mine.

Her pussy is mine, and now it's time to fucking claim it.

She's breathing hard as she watches me crawl over her, caging her body beneath mine. She's so small and perfect, and when her thighs part to welcome me between them, my chest tightens.

"So good," I murmur. "Such a good girl."

I settle between her legs, propping myself up on one arm while I reach down to guide my cock to her entrance. Her slick little hole is wet and ready for me, and when the head nudges against her, I have to grit my teeth to keep from losing control.

I rub the crown of my dick through her folds, teasing her. Making her squirm.

And when I finally start to push inside, the feeling is indescribable.

She's so fucking tight. Too tight. Her virgin pussy is a hot, velvety vice, gripping me hard.

But I'm not stopping.

She whimpers and shifts beneath me, and her body yields, taking a little more. Then a little more.

She's making tiny noises, little pained sounds, but her hips shift and rock, like she's chasing the sensation.

"Shhh, babygirl," I croon. "It's alright. It'll get better soon."

"It hurts."

"I know. But you're taking it so well. Almost there."

I push forward again, and then her gasp turns into a moan as I finally sink all the way inside her.

"Good girl," I rasp. "You did it."

She's trembling now, her legs wrapped around me and her fingers digging into my biceps. "God, it's... so much."

"Your tight little pussy feels so good, babygirl. Made for me. Made to take my cock."

She's breathing fast, but she's relaxing around me. Growing used to the size. The fullness.

I move slowly, sliding out and then pushing back in. The drag of her walls against my shaft makes me lightheaded, and when her breathy whimpers turn into moans, I feel like a fucking god.

"That's it," I say, leaning down to nip her ear. "That's a good girl."

I start a rhythm, pumping into her with long, deep strokes. Each one is more perfect than the last, and her whimpers quickly turn into gasps.

"Yes. More. Please, Jack."

Jesus.

I give it to her. Thrusting into her over and over, hard enough to make her tits bounce. Hard enough to make the bed shake and groan beneath us. My free hand moves to her breasts, squeezing one tit roughly and groaning as a warm spray of milk hits my chest.

I do it again, soaking myself with her sweet cream while her pussy grips me and her moans echo off the walls.

"You're so fucking perfect," I tell her. "Look at you, taking my cock. Taking all of me. You're so good. Such a good girl. But I need to fill you now. Need to plant my seed inside you and get you pregnant."

She whines, high-pitched and needy. "Please. Please."

I thrust harder. Deeper. I'm grunting and cursing, and she's clawing at my arms, her heels digging into my back and her breath coming in ragged little pants.

Then I reach a hand down between us, my fingers searching for the little bud and rubbing it in firm circles.

"That's it," I growl. "That's it, babygirl. Come for me. Soak me. Make my cock slick. Let me breed you."

Her nails dig into my shoulders as her entire body tightens, and I feel the pulse of her orgasm. Her release, clenching and squeezing around my cock, like she's begging for my cum.

And then I can't hold back anymore.

The world goes hazy. My pulse roars in my ears, and all I can feel is the rush of my release as it shoots out of me, filling her, painting her insides. Coating her. Claiming her.

Mine.

Jenna cries out, clinging to me like her life depends on it, and the sound makes my head spin.

My hips stutter, and I thrust through my release, groaning and cursing and saying her name.

"That's it, babygirl," I grunt. "Take it all, Jenna. Take every fucking drop."

Then I collapse, holding her close and pressing my face into the crook of her neck. Her scent is all around me, and her hair is soft against my skin.

"I love you," I say, voice raw. "I love you so much, Jenna."

"I love you too," she whispers, her lips brushing my ear.

My heart aches and swells and pounds, and I tighten my arms around her.

We're a mess. Damp with sweat and slick with our release. But neither of us moves. We just stay there, tangled together in a warm heap. I can't even bear to pull out of her, wanting to keep her plugged with my cock so my seed can't escape.

And as I bring my mouth to her nipple, taking it into my mouth and sucking until her sweet milk begins to flow, I know I'll never get enough of this.

Of her.

Forever isn't going to be anywhere near long enough.

Epilogue

Jack

My palms are sweaty and my heart is thundering as I rise to my feet at the front of the church, taking my cue from the way the music suddenly grows louder.

I turn to look down the aisle, waiting for my bride to appear.

I've already seen her dress, already kissed her swollen belly this morning, already tasted the honey-sweet milk she let down just for me before we left for the venue.

But nothing could have prepared me for this.

She steps into view, and I stop breathing.

Jenna Lane is walking down the aisle towards me, glowing like the sun, one hand cradling the soft curve of the belly I put there. My baby growing inside my bride. Her other hand holds a simple bouquet of ivory roses, and behind her, Grace trails along in her pale pink maid-of-honor gown, tears already gathering in her eyes.

But everyone else in the room fades to nothing.

I only see Jenna.

I see the woman I worship. The body I claimed. The future I've anchored myself to with every touch, every word, every drop of my seed she's taken inside her.

And somehow, between growing our baby and keeping me completely wrapped around her finger, she still plans weddings like it's her superpower. She's booked out months in advance, with clients demanding to work with her, and she makes every bride feel like royalty.

Mine.

The thought pulses through me like a war drum.

Mine. Mine. Mine.

And it's not just her soft mouth or her sweet curves or the way she melts when I call her my good girl.

It's this. This moment. That dress clinging to her swollen belly. Her cheeks flushed. Her eyes locked on mine.

She's proud. She's radiant. She's carrying my fucking baby. And I'm about to give her my last name too.

My throat tightens.

God, she's beautiful.

She's not nervous. Not even close. She floats down the aisle like she knows exactly who she belongs to. Like she wants everyone in this room to know what I've done to her. That I filled her up and bred her deep and kept her by my side ever since.

I curl my hands into fists, letting my nails dig into my palms to keep myself grounded. If I move right now, I'll run straight down that aisle and pull her into my arms.

I won't make it through this ceremony without thinking about what she tastes like. What her breasts feel like when they are full and heavy in my palms. How her voice goes high and breathy when I stroke her stomach and tell her I want to give her another baby the moment this one's born.

I should be thinking about vows and rings and holy matrimony.

But instead, all I can think is: *She's mine. And she'll never belong to anyone else.*

Not when I've marked her so deeply. Not when my baby is growing inside her. Not when I've claimed her in every possible way a man can.

And when she's finally standing in front of me, eyes wide and shining, her belly gently pressing against me as I take her hands in mine...

All I want to do is fall to my knees and worship.

Forever.

About the Author

♥

Welcome to my wild, wicked world of *over-the-top, heart-pounding instalove*. I write fast-paced, **spicy age gap novellas** that don't waste time. They are just pure heat, obsession, and unapologetic desire from page one. If you're into dominant older heroes, eager younger heroines, and deliciously deviant themes like **breeding** and **lactation**, you're in the right place.

These days, all my stories revolve around one irresistible idea: **men who fall fast, fall hard, and never let go**. Think possessive, primal, borderline unhinged alphas who'd burn the world down for their girl. They're obsessed, they're intense, and yes, more than one has been lovingly described as a full-blown *caveman* by reviewers.

So whether you're here for the age gaps, the obsession, or the kind of heat that leaves scorch marks, you're in the right place. Get comfortable. It's about to get *feral*.

Find me online at https://allmylinks.com/willow-watkins

Printed in Dunstable, United Kingdom

71046849R00037